To
_____

From
_____

Date
_____

WHAT GOD SAYS ABOUT YOU

HOSANNA WONG

ILLUSTRATED BY
LIZ BRIZZI

An Imprint of Thomas Nelson

What God Says About You

© 2025 by Hosanna Wong

Tommy Nelson, PO Box 141000, Nashville, TN 37214

All rights reserved. No portion of this book may be reproduced, stored in a retrieval system, or transmitted in any form or by any means—electronic, mechanical, photocopy, recording, scanning, or other—except for brief quotations in critical reviews or articles, without the prior written permission of the publisher.

Published in Nashville, Tennessee, by Tommy Nelson. Tommy Nelson is an imprint of Thomas Nelson. Thomas Nelson is a registered trademark of HarperCollins Christian Publishing, Inc.

Author is represented by Jenni Burke of Illuminate Literary Agency, www.illluminateliterary.com.

Tommy Nelson titles may be purchased in bulk for educational, business, fundraising, or sales promotional use. For information, please email SpecialMarkets@ThomasNelson.com.

Scripture quotations marked CEV are taken from the Contemporary English Version. Copyright © 1991, 1992, 1995 by American Bible Society. Used by permission.

Scripture quotations marked NIV are taken from the Holy Bible, New International Version®, NIV®. Copyright © 1973, 1978, 1984, 2011 by Biblica, Inc.® Used by permission of Zondervan. All rights reserved worldwide. www.zondervan.com. The "NIV" and "New International Version" are trademarks registered in the United States Patent and Trademark Office by Biblica, Inc.®

Scripture quotations marked NLT are taken from the Holy Bible, New Living Translation. Copyright © 1996, 2004, 2015 by Tyndale House Foundation. Used by permission of Tyndale House Publishers, Carol Stream, Illinois 60188. All rights reserved.

ISBN 978-1-4002-5565-8 (audiobook)
ISBN 978-1-4002-5129-2 (eBook)
ISBN 978-1-4002-5128-5 (HC)

Library of Congress Control Number: 2025003445

Written by Hosanna Wong

Illustrated by Liz Brizzi

Printed in Malaysia
25 26 27 28 29 OFF 5 4 3 2 1

Mfr: OFF / Batu Tiga, Malaysia / July 2025 / PO #12317384

To my mom. Thank you for reading the most wonderful books to me when I was growing up. It was always my dream to write one and get to read it to you. This one is for you.

—YOUR FAVORITE KID (AT LEAST TOP 3)

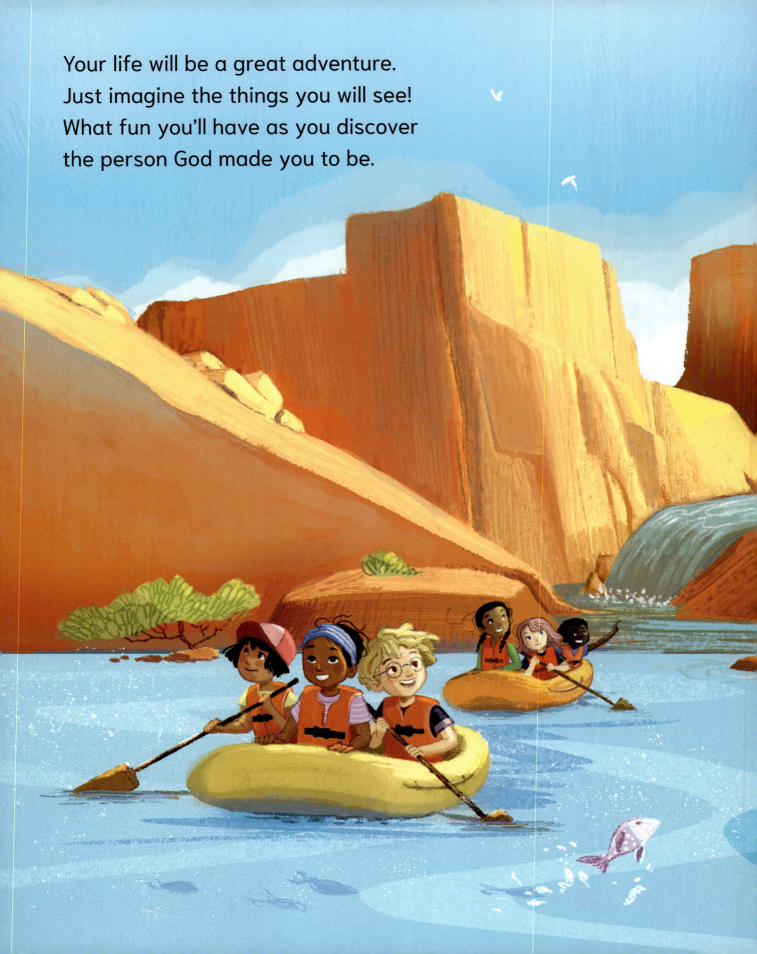

Your life will be a great adventure. Just imagine the things you will see! What fun you'll have as you discover the person God made you to be.

No matter where you choose to go,
the people you meet, or the things you do,
it's important that you always know
the wonderful things God says about you!

Has someone ever called you a name?
Or said something really unkind?
Others may call you a thing that you're not,
so it's important to know what is right!

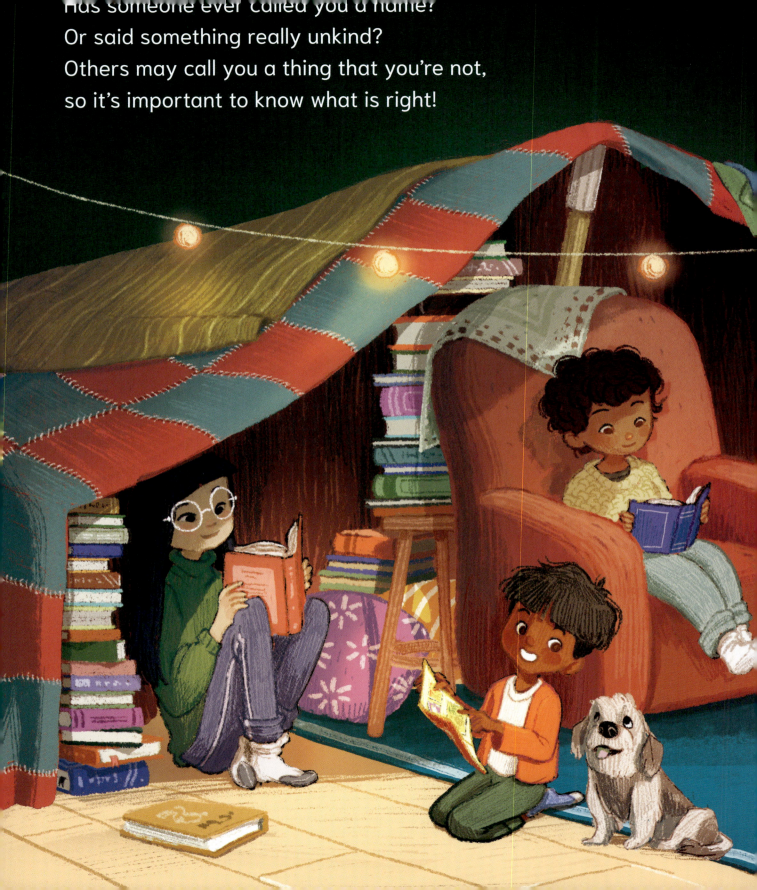

And who gets to name a thing, anyway?
Why, of course, the creator who made it!
So everything God says about you
is final and true—you can't change it!

If you're wondering about who you are
or what you've been made to do,
keep your head high and remind yourself of
these truths that God says about you.

God loves when you spend time together.
You can talk to Him wherever you are.
Your feelings, your hurts, your hopes—*share them all!*
He's always available and never far.

With God as your friend, you are never alone.
He'll always stay close by your side.
So when you are young and as you grow old,
He'll be with you for the whole ride.

"WHO AM I? I AM GOD'S FRIEND!"

God made each of His kids with a purpose for a certain time and a certain place. God chose *you* to be *here* for this very moment.
You are *important* for the world He made.

He picked *you* to show people His love, and that happens in all kinds of ways—from sharing a toy to saying kind words or inviting a new friend to play!

"WHO AM I? I AM CHOSEN!"

The God who created you is an artist.
You're a one-of-a-kind work of art.
Each of your details was handmade on purpose.
God happily crafted each part.

GOD'S

MASTERPIECE

He loves your sparkling eyes and smile.
He gave your nose its special shape.
If ever you wonder if you're amazing,
   just think,
I'm exactly what God wanted to make!

"WHO AM I? I AM GOD'S MASTERPIECE!"

All our bodies are good and important.
They come in all shapes and sizes.
And you know what's amazing?
　　Your body's a home!
And God's Spirit lives inside it.

GOD'S TEMPLE

The mirror shows your wonderful outside.
But remember your inside's amazing too.
Take good care of your body
  and be kind to yourself.
You honor God and yourself when you do.

"WHO AM I? I AM GOD'S TEMPLE!"

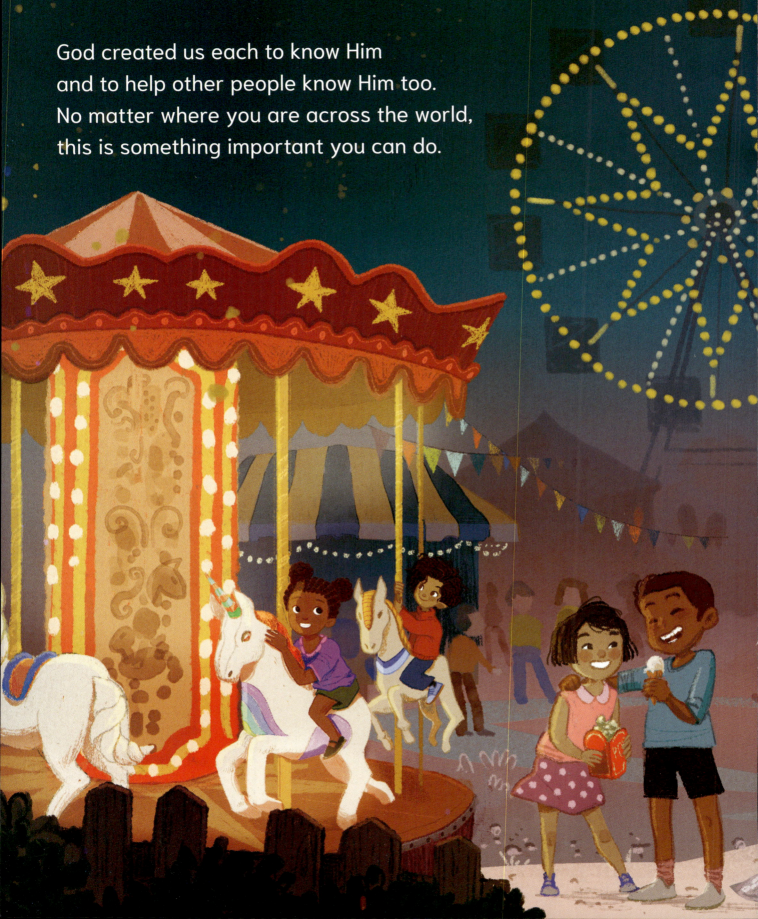

God created us each to know Him
and to help other people know Him too.
No matter where you are across the world,
this is something important you can do.

Tell others the wonderful names God calls them.
Reveal who He is and share what He's done.
They may never have heard they're loved and chosen.
You may be the first person they hear that from.

"WHO AM I? I AM GOD'S MESSENGER!"

Sometimes it's hard to know where you fit, the place where you truly and fully belong. This name means you're *not a visitor or guest*— you're *an important part* of the family of God.

CHILD OF GOD

Throughout your life you may be lots of things—
an artist, athlete, pilot, or nurse.
Whether a teacher, a chef, or a million other dreams,
you will always be God's child *first*.

"WHO AM I? I AM A CHILD OF GOD!"

GREATLY

Like the endless sky, God's love has no limits.
He loves you more than you can measure
or guess.
Nothing you do could make God love
you *more*.
And nothing could make Him love you *less*.

If you ever feel lonely or misunderstood
or left out or unloved, then know this:
God knows you the best and loves you the most.
In unseen moments, you're still seen by Him!

"WHO AM I? I AM GREATLY LOVED!"

When you do something wrong or make a mistake,
you don't have to feel bad for too long.
Once you admit it and tell God you're sorry,
He forgives you and helps you move on.

Like a bird in a cage that's released to the sky,
God sets you free from guilt and shame.
You're not defined by what you did wrong.
Free, Indeed is your new name.

"WHO AM I? I AM FREE, INDEED!"

Have you ever felt like you chose the wrong path?
Is there something you want to redo?
Don't let mistakes make you feel there's no hope.
God *loves* turning old into new.

God makes miracles from scratch
   and grows flowers from dirt.
He cares about what hurts your heart,
and He wants to heal it and help it grow strong.
God *loves* to give you a fresh start.

"WHO AM I? I AM BRAND NEW!"

As you journey through your life,
    you'll be called *many names*—
some silly, some snarky, some true.
But no one has the power
    to give you your *true name*
except for God, who created you.

As you travel along the road of life,
when you're home or at school or afar,
remember the names that God's given you.
They'll remind you who you truly are!

God calls all His children these names!
Echo His words and do just the same!

Tell others what God calls them too!
Today, what name sticks out to YOU?

GOD'S FRIEND

"I have called you friends, for everything that I learned from my Father I have made known to you."

JOHN 15:15 NIV

CHOSEN

"For we know, brothers and sisters loved by God, that he has chosen you . . ."

1 THESSALONIANS 1:4 NIV

GOD'S MASTERPIECE

"For we are God's masterpiece. He has created us anew in Christ Jesus, so we can do the good things he planned for us long ago."

EPHESIANS 2:10 NLT

GOD'S TEMPLE

"You surely know that your body is a temple where the Holy Spirit lives. The Spirit is in you and is a gift from God."

1 CORINTHIANS 6:19 CEV

HI! I'M HOSANNA! My favorite things are eating noodles, dancing with friends, playing basketball, and reading comic books with my brother. I also love writing! When I was little, I would write poems and stories and give them as gifts. Now I write books and share stories about God all over the world! I especially love talking about the wonderful names God calls us. And I hope this book reminds you that you are who God says you are. God loves all your fun details, and He loves YOU!